Wizards Don't
Wear Graduation
Gowns

There are more books about the Bailey School kids!
Have you read these adventures?

Wizards Don't Wear Graduation Gowns

by Debbie Dadey
and
Marcia Thornton Jones

illustrated by John Steven Gurney

A
LITTLE APPLE
PAPERBACK

SCHOLASTIC INC.
New York   Toronto   London   Auckland   Sydney
Mexico City   New Delhi   Hong Kong   Buenos Aires

For Brantley
and
Hannah Rosenfeld
— MTJ

To Justin, Christina, and Sean Pellman —
great neighbors.
— DD

ISBN 0-439-36803-0

Text copyright © 2002 by Marcia Thornton Jones and Debra S. Dadey. Illustrations copyright © 2002 by Scholastic Inc. SCHOLASTIC, LITTLE APPLE PAPERBACKS, THE ADVENTURES OF THE BAILEY SCHOOL KIDS, and associated logos are trademarks and/or registered trademarks of Scholastic Inc.

12 11 10 9 8 7 6 5 4   2 3 4 5 6 7/0

Printed in the U.S.A.   40
First Scholastic printing, March 2002

Contents

1

Summer Magic

"Yippee!" Eddie sang. "It's the last week of school!" He threw his ball cap into the air and it caught on a low tree branch.

Eddie and his friends Melody, Liza, and Howie stood under the giant oak tree near the Bailey School playground. The branches were loaded with bright green leaves, but the kids were still able to see Eddie's blue cap. Eddie climbed into the branches to grab it.

"Summer is magic," Howie said. "We can do anything we want. I'm going to spend my summer reading books."

Liza smiled. "I'm going to take a class at the Arts and Crafts Center. I'll weave a bookmark for you."

Eddie hopped down from the tree and landed between his friends. "Boring," he

said. "Summer is for doing exciting stuff. That's why I'm going to soccer camp."

"You're lucky," Liza said. "I heard soccer camp was already full."

Eddie slapped his ball cap over his curly red hair and grinned. "My grandmother signed me up months ago! I'm playing in a tournament this Saturday with the kids going to the camp. I'll be their best player."

Liza sighed. "Soccer is a team sport," she reminded Eddie. "There is no *I* in the word *team*."

"I wish I could go," Melody said. "My mom called to sign me up, but the camp was already full."

"That's terrible," Liza said, patting Melody on the shoulder. "You can go to the Arts Center with me," she offered.

Melody shook her head so hard her black braids swung from side to side. "Don't worry about me. I found something even better than soccer."

Eddie put his hands on his hips. "What could be better than soccer?" he asked.

"Rock climbing!" Melody said with a grin.

"Rock climbing?" her friends all said at the same time.

"Yep," Melody said. "I'm going to learn how to scale cliffs."

"That sounds dangerous," Liza said.

"Too dangerous," Eddie said, "for a girl."

"What's that supposed to mean?" Melody asked. She was no longer smiling. Now her eyes squinted in an angry frown.

Eddie shrugged. "Everyone knows rock climbing isn't a sport for girls. It takes muscles and brains to climb mountains."

"It also takes practice and perseverance," Melody said, taking a step closer to Eddie. "I have everything it takes to be a rock climber!"

Howie jumped between his friends just as a huge bird floated across the sky and settled in the branches right over their heads.

"Is that a hawk?" Liza gasped.

"If it is, it's the biggest hawk I've ever seen," Howie whispered.

The bird hopped down to a lower branch, its sharp talons digging into the bark. It tilted its head, locking its beady eyes on the kids.

"I don't like the way it's looking at me," Liza whimpered.

"Me, neither," Eddie said, taking a step away from the tree. "It's as if that bird is listening to every word we're saying."

"I think it's wondering how we'd taste for breakfast," Liza whispered.

"Let's get out of here!" Melody shrieked and raced toward the school. Her three friends weren't the only ones that followed. The hawk screeched, spread its wings, and took flight. It swooped through the air, right after them.

"RUN!" Howie screamed.

Unfortunately, the kids weren't fast enough.

2

Madge Jhick

The four kids rushed inside the school and crashed into a strange woman, knocking her books to the floor. "Whoopsy daisy," she said. The woman wore a purple dress covered with shiny stars. Thick round glasses made her green eyes look like giant olives.

"We're sorry," Melody panted. Melody and Howie bent down to pick up the lady's things. They were surprised to find the books had landed in a nice, neat pile.

"Mighty stars," the woman said. "What has scared you so?"

Liza gasped for air and pointed out the door. "Swooped down . . . to eat . . . giant bird," she panted.

The stranger's eyes got even bigger behind her thick glasses, and she clutched an amber-colored stone that dangled from

a chain around her neck. "You swooped from a tree and ate a giant bird? What kind of school is this?"

"No, that's not what she meant," Howie said, handing the stranger her books. "There was a bird in the tree."

"It swooped down," Melody added.

"To eat us," Eddie said.

The stranger's laugh sounded like chimes in the wind. "Little birds don't nibble on children," she said.

Eddie did not like being laughed at. "This was not a little bird," he snapped.

"Be nice," Liza whispered.

"I am being nice," Eddie said. "Just take a look at that monster bird!"

The stranger peered through a window to where Eddie pointed. The bird was settling into the top branches of the oak tree. The stranger laughed again. "You have nothing to fear from that majestic hawk. Even though it is a bird of prey, it would not find children appetizing."

The lady fluttered her fingers in the direction of the bird as if it was nothing at all. Just then, a breeze rustled the leaves of the tree. The hawk ruffled its feathers and spread its wings. It took off and soared so close to the door the kids could see its black eyes staring right at them. Then, as if waving, the bird flapped its wings and disappeared from view.

"There," the woman said, "nothing to worry about."

"My name is Liza and these are my friends Howie, Melody, and Eddie." Liza reached out to shake hands, but stopped when she saw the stone dangling from the stranger's neck. The stone was the color of a cat's eye and looked as if it was staring straight at the kids. Liza stepped to the right and left. The stone's eye followed her.

The stranger didn't seem to notice Liza dancing from side to side in front of her. "It's lovely to meet you," the woman told the children. "My name is Mrs. Jhick.

Madge Jhick. I am here to train for the job of assistant principal."

"What's wrong with our old principal?" Eddie blurted. "Is he sick?"

Mrs. Jhick smiled. "Of course not. I'm hoping to be a principal next year, and Principal Davis agreed to teach me everything he knows. Besides, he has his hands full with so many students and the upcoming graduation ceremony. I can help. And the first thing I plan to do is make sure students get to class on time."

Then, with a gentle flick of her wrist, Mrs. Jhick waved the kids off to class. Before Liza turned to leave, she glanced at Mrs. Jhick's necklace one more time. Then Liza looked up into Mrs. Jhick's face.

The assistant principal's eyes were big behind her thick glasses. "Remember," she told Liza. "I'll be keeping an eye on you and your friends!"

3

Mortimer

Mrs. Jeepers, the kids' third-grade teacher, was already writing multiplication problems on the board when Melody, Eddie, Howie, and Liza slipped into their desks.

"Why do we have to do schoolwork?" Eddie grumbled. "School is almost over. We should be able to have recess all day for the entire week."

"Shh," Melody whispered with a finger to her lips. She looked toward Mrs. Jeepers to make sure their teacher hadn't heard.

Mrs. Jeepers was not an ordinary teacher. In fact, most kids believed she was a vampire from Transylvania and that the green brooch she wore at her throat was magic. They didn't dare make her angry. Of course, Eddie was not most kids.

Eddie waved his hand high in the air and waited for Mrs. Jeepers to call on him.

"I can't see over Howie's head," Eddie told his teacher, "so I can't do the math." Eddie crossed his arms, slid down in his chair, and grinned.

Mrs. Jeepers' eyes flashed at Eddie. Then she smiled a little half smile. "You may sit in Morty's desk today," she said in her Transylvanian accent. "You will be able to see the board from there."

"But Morty needs his desk," Eddie argued.

"Not today," Mrs. Jeepers said. "He will not be joining us for the rest of the year."

The class stared at the empty desk in the front of the room where Morty usually sat. Morty wasn't really a bad kid, but he did tend to get on people's nerves. He had a habit of chewing all the erasers off pencils, and he was a champion tattletale.

"Where is Morty?" Liza asked as Eddie stomped to Morty's desk.

Mrs. Jeepers shrugged. "I understand he has flown away," she said, turning back to the chalkboard.

"I'm glad he's gone," Eddie whispered with a snicker. "Now he can't tattle on me. It's the perfect time to cause a little mischief."

"You better behave and do your math," Melody whispered as Eddie walked by her. If there was one thing Eddie didn't want to do, it was math.

He looked around. The rest of the class had their heads bent over their work. Mrs. Jeepers was busy grading papers. Eddie scooted his sneakers across the floor. A satisfying squeak caused a few kids to look up, but then they went right back to work.

Eddie reached inside Morty's desk. The desk was empty of books, but some scraps of paper and a few pencils were still there. Eddie grabbed the pencils, made sure Mrs. Jeepers wasn't looking, and then put the pencils under his top lip to make two long fangs hanging down on either side of his chin. He looked to his right until a girl named Carey glanced up. She rolled her eyes at Eddie and went back to work.

No one else paid a bit of attention to him. This was going to require drastic action. Eddie reached all the way to the back of Morty's desk. There, in the corner, he found just what he wanted. A handful of eraser pieces bitten off Morty's pencils.

Eddie lined them up on the desk and flicked the erasers across the room. Tiny eraser bombs sailed through the air.

Plop. One landed on Liza's desk.

Ping. Another one landed on Howie's math book.

THUD. A third one landed right on top of Mrs. Jeepers' head.

Melody gasped. Liza closed her eyes.

Howie's face turned as pale as his math paper.

Mrs. Jeepers plucked the piece of eraser from her long red hair. Her eyes flashed at Eddie, and she gently touched the green brooch at her throat.

"I have had enough," she said in a very soft voice, but it was loud enough for everyone to hear. "Eddie, please leave at once and go to the principal's office."

Eddie slid from Morty's desk and left the room without looking at his friends.

When Eddie got to the office, Mr. Davis, the principal, was busy talking on the phone and the secretary was in the middle of putting a bandage on a kindergartner's knee. She didn't bother asking Eddie why he was there. Mrs. Lucky was used to seeing Eddie in the office. "You'll have to see the assistant principal today," Mrs. Lucky said in a very tired voice.

Mrs. Jhick stood up from her desk when Eddie knocked on her door. As she did, she tripped on her chair and sent a stack of papers fluttering to the floor. "Whoopsy daisy," she said.

Eddie stooped to pick up the papers, hoping they were full of school secrets. He was disappointed to see they were nothing but recipes.

"Please have a seat," Mrs. Jhick said.

Eddie froze. There, perched in the corner, was the last thing he expected to see in the school's office. A crow with rumpled feathers clung to the curtains.

19

"I see you've noticed Mortimer," Mrs. Jhick said. "Please don't be frightened."

Eddie swallowed. "Me?" he said. His voice squeaked just a little. "I'm not afraid of a little bird."

"Scrarwk!" the bird said. It flapped its wings and landed on Mrs. Jhick's desk.

"Now, tell me what happened," the assistant principal asked.

Eddie breathed a sigh of relief. Obviously, this lady didn't know the real story.

"I didn't do a thing," Eddie lied. "I was just in the wrong place at the wrong time."

Mortimer interrupted him with a loud "Scrarwk!" Then the crow ruffled his feathers and hopped over to the arm of Eddie's chair. Eddie scooted as far away as possible.

"What were you saying?" Mrs. Jhick urged.

Eddie swallowed hard. He didn't like the way the bird's little black eyes

gleamed at him. Eddie looked away, focusing on Mrs. Jhick instead. "I didn't do a thing," he lied again. "It's a case of mistaken identity."

"SCRARWK!" Mortimer's cry interrupted Eddie again. This time the bird hopped up on Eddie's head. Eddie didn't dare move. He also didn't dare lie again. Eddie had no choice. He told Mrs. Jhick the truth.

4

And the Winner Is . . .

"Go, Melody!" Liza cheered for her best friend. It was recess time, and Melody easily won the race against Huey and Carey.

"Anyone else want to race?" Melody asked, panting after running so fast.

Howie and Liza shook their heads along with Huey and Carey. "You're too fast for us," Howie admitted.

"Maybe Eddie will race you when he gets back from the principal's office," Liza suggested.

Melody stared at the school door. "What is taking Eddie so long?" she asked. "I hope he didn't get in too much trouble."

"Uh-oh," Liza said. "Here he comes now and he doesn't look happy."

Eddie stormed out the back door and

glared at his friends. "What are you guys looking at?" he snapped.

Melody folded her arms over her chest and dared Eddie to race her. "Bet you can't beat me in a race."

"Oh, yes I can," Eddie said. "Beating you is just what I need to turn this day around. A boy can beat a girl with one hand behind his back."

"That's crazy," Melody sputtered. "Girls are faster than boys!"

Howie stood between his friends. "There's only one way to settle this argument," he told them. "Get ready. Get set. Go!"

Melody and Eddie took off like they'd been blasted out of a cannon. "Go, Melody!" Liza screamed. Other girls on the playground stopped jumping rope and cheered for Melody. All the boys yelled for Eddie to win.

"It's going to be a tie!" Howie shouted, but that was before a big black hawk swooped right above Eddie's and Melody's heads.

"Look out!" Liza screamed. Melody was too intent on winning to notice the bird, but Eddie ducked. That was all that Melody needed. She darted ahead and crossed the finish line first.

"I won!" Melody screamed. She jumped up and down along with all the other girls on the playground. "I proved girls are faster than boys!"

"You did no such thing," Eddie said, waving his fist at the hawk as it soared away. "I would have won if that bird hadn't tried to eat my ears for lunch!" he yelled.

"Don't tell me you're afraid of a little bird," Carey said with a snicker.

"I am not afraid of a bird," Eddie said. "But you should have seen the one in Mrs. Jhick's office. It was the strangest bird I've ever seen."

Carey and the other kids were not im-

pressed by Eddie's story. They wandered off, leaving Howie, Liza, Melody, and Eddie alone.

"Mrs. Jhick has a bird in her office?" Liza asked. "That's weird."

Eddie nodded. "This bird is more than weird. It's a loudmouthed, rumpled crow named Mortimer."

Melody wiped sweat from her forehead. "I think it's neat that Mrs. Jhick has a bird. Maybe she's an animal rescuer and she saved Mortimer."

"What's that?" Eddie asked. "Animal 911?"

Liza giggled, but Melody was serious. "I read in the paper about animal rescuers making new homes for falcons on tall buildings, bridges, and even cliffs."

"Why don't they just leave the stupid birds alone?" Eddie said.

Melody rolled her eyes. "Because the birds' habitats have been taken away by people building cities and the birds need new places to live."

"I think your brains have been taken away," Eddie said. "Birds can just fly someplace else and live. They don't need any help."

"Oh, Eddie," Melody complained, "sometimes you can be more irritating than a crowing rooster."

Eddie opened his mouth, ready to say more, but a big white hand squeezed his shoulder. For the first time in his life, Eddie was speechless.

5

Evil Eye

Melody gulped as Mrs. Jhick stood before the kids. Mrs. Jhick held her strange amber necklace in her hand. Something about it captured the kids' attention. They couldn't tear their eyes away from the unusual stone that looked like a cat's eye. The kids didn't even notice the bird perched high above them in the oak tree.

Liza shivered. Mrs. Jhick's necklace scared her right down to her dirty socks. Liza had never seen a piece of jewelry that stared back at her.

"Friends like you shouldn't say such words to one another," Mrs. Jhick told Melody and Eddie. The four friends nodded and kept staring at the stone. Mrs. Jhick continued, "Angry words make you sorry afterward. Before you speak, you

must think twice. Boys and girls should always be nice."

Huey accidentally kicked a ball toward Eddie, and Mrs. Jhick turned away from the kids. "Huey," Mrs. Jhick told him, "you must be more careful." Huey nodded, grabbed his ball, and ran to line up.

"Hurry back inside," Mrs. Jhick said to the four friends. "Your class is due in the gym in exactly seven minutes and thirty-two seconds."

After Mrs. Jhick went inside, Melody shook her head to get the cat's eye out of her mind. "That necklace gives me the creeps," Melody admitted. "I wonder where Mrs. Jhick got something so strange."

"A strange necklace for a strange lady," Howie said softly.

Liza giggled. "Mrs. Jhick doesn't know Eddie very well. He doesn't think once before opening his mouth."

Eddie looked at Liza and opened his mouth. Liza braced herself for one of

Eddie's smart aleck comments. It never came.

Instead, Eddie smiled and patted Liza on the back. "You know, Liza," Eddie said, "sometimes you are so right."

Liza stared at Eddie like his face had sprouted a crocodile nose. She put her hand on Eddie's forehead. "Are you feeling all right?" she asked.

Melody leaned back against the oak tree. Eddie never ceased to amaze her. She never knew what he would do next.

Howie stared at Eddie, too. Even when the rest of the kids lined up to go inside, Howie continued to stare. Something was not right, and Howie knew exactly what it was.

6

Great Honor

"We have to do what?" Eddie complained. He was sitting on the gymnasium bleachers with all the other third graders. Mrs. Jeepers stood on the wooden floor facing them.

Their teacher frowned at Eddie and repeated what she had just told the third graders. "This Saturday you are all invited to sing at the sixth-grade graduation ceremony. It is a great honor. You will sing the school graduation song. We shall practice it now."

The kids stood up and began singing:

"Oh, Bailey School, we love you so,
With you in our hearts
*   we'll ever go . . ."*

Actually, Eddie sang something a bit different. His song went more like this:

"Oh, Bailey School, you stink so so,
With you we'll throw up high and
*   low . . ."*

"Eddie," Liza hissed as the other kids continued to sing. "You shouldn't be so rude. This is an important occasion for the sixth graders."

"I don't care about graduations," Eddie whispered back. "My soccer tournament is this Saturday. My team is depending on me."

"Shh," Howie told his friends. "Here comes Mrs. Jhick."

"Now you're in trouble," Melody said. "She probably heard you singing the wrong words."

But Mrs. Jhick didn't walk over to Eddie. She went to speak to Mrs. Jeepers instead. Mrs. Jhick had changed into a long, flowing black robe, and it was hard

to tell if she was flying or walking. It almost looked like Mrs. Jhick was floating.

"What kind of dumb getup is that?" Eddie asked.

"That's a graduation gown," Liza told Eddie. "Everyone wears them at graduation ceremonies."

"Humph," Eddie said. "It looks more like a nightgown to me."

Mrs. Jhick finished talking to Mrs. Jeepers and turned to face the kids. The cat's-eye necklace glared at Howie. Howie stared until something made him jump.

Howie blinked three times. Did the new assistant principal's necklace really wink at him?

7

Reading, Math, and Spells

Howie didn't say much for the rest of the day. He kept imagining Mrs. Jhick's necklace winking at him.

"Are you okay?" Liza asked Howie when they gathered under the oak tree after school. The spring sun beat down on them, and a breeze whispered through the leaves overhead.

Howie shrugged. "I've been thinking . . ."

Eddie didn't let Howie finish. "I've been thinking, too. And it makes me mad," Eddie said. "We shouldn't have to go to that goofy graduation. I already had plans to play in the soccer tournament and now they're ruined, thanks to Mrs. Madge Jhick."

Howie stared at his friend. "W-w-what did you say?" he stammered.

"You heard me," Eddie griped and kicked his stuffed book bag. "Not only that, we shouldn't have to do homework. It's the last week of school, and Mrs. Jeepers is making us do three pages of math and read an entire book. I bet she's planning a spelling test on Friday, too!"

Howie's mouth dropped open. "S-s-spells?" he stuttered.

Eddie put a hand on Howie's shoulder. "See, you agree," Eddie said. "Homework wouldn't be so bad if it was raining, but just look up. Nothing but blue skies. A perfect day for a little soccer practice. Someone might as well turn this sunny day into thunderstorms and rain for all the good it's doing us."

Liza pushed a loose strand of blonde hair from her face and pointed a finger at Eddie. "You should try being more positive. All you ever do is complain."

"That's true," Melody added. "Haven't you learned that complaining doesn't do any good?"

"Eddie doesn't always have bad things to say," Howie said in a whisper. "After all, he hasn't insulted any of us this afternoon!"

"What do you mean?" Melody asked. "Eddie is a natural-born smart aleck. He always insults us."

Howie shook his head. "Not since Mrs. Jhick talked to him. Remember? She warned Eddie to think twice and to always be nice."

"Hey," Liza said, "that rhymes."

Howie slowly nodded. "So you know, too?"

"Know what?" Eddie demanded.

Howie put his hand on Eddie's sleeve. "Thanks to Eddie and the things he just said, I figured it out."

"You're making about as much sense as Mrs. Jhick's silly bird," Eddie said.

"Exactly," Howie said. "It makes perfect sense. Mrs. Jhick is not an assistant principal at all. She's a wizard!"

8

Wizettes

Melody smiled. Liza giggled. Eddie sat down on the ground and laughed.

"Mrs. Jhick can't be a wizard," Liza explained. "They don't wear graduation gowns."

"Liza is right," Melody said. "Wizards don't save wild animals, either."

"And wizards definitely aren't girls!" Eddie blurted from his seat on the grass.

Melody bent over and poked Eddie in the chest. "What is that supposed to mean?" she demanded.

Eddie hopped up from the ground. "Simple. Wizards are tough and can make all sorts of magic, like Merlin in King Arthur's day. Have you ever heard of a wizard that was a woman?"

Melody's mouth was set in a straight line and she put her hands on her hips.

"Girls can do anything boys can do. They can be doctors, or lawyers, or astronauts. Girls can beat boys in races, and they can even be wizards."

"Women can't be wizards, but maybe they can be wizettes," Eddie teased.

"If Mrs. Jhick wants to be a wizard, then she can be a wizard!" Liza said, interrupting Eddie.

Howie stepped between his friends. "We don't want Mrs. Jhick to be a wizard," he warned, "and it has nothing to do with whether she's a girl or a boy."

"First of all," Eddie said, "Mrs. Jhick is not a wizard because there are no such things as wizards. But if there were, I think having a wizard around could come in very handy. Just think, with a wave of a wizard's wand, all our homework could disappear!"

Howie looked each of his friends in the eyes. "That's true, but think about it. What do you know about wizards?" Howie asked.

"They cook up potions," Liza said.

"If they were real, they would say magic spells," Eddie said.

"They use crystal balls and magic stones," Melody added.

"Wizards create powerful magic with all those things. They talk to animals, too," Howie told them. "They can even convince animals to do their magic for them."

Just then, a loud "scrarwk" interrupted them. The four kids looked up. Perched high in the branches above them was Mortimer.

Mortimer ruffled his feathers and cocked his head. "Scrarwk!" Mortimer shrieked one more time before spreading his wings and flying back toward the school.

"Do you think Mortimer is going to tell Mrs. Jhick we know she's a wizard?" Howie asked with a hoarse voice.

"Of course not," Eddie said, "because Mortimer is just an ordinary crow."

Howie shook his head. "You're wrong," he said, his voice trembling. "Mortimer isn't a crow at all, and Mrs. Jhick isn't an ordinary assistant principal!"

9

A Magic Name

"If what Howie says is true," Liza said slowly, "then wizards would have enough magic to change people into animals . . . Oh, my gosh! Isn't Mortimer another name for Morty?"

Melody nodded. "Morty is a nickname for Mortimer."

"If Howie is right and Mrs. Jhick is really a wizard, then maybe she turned poor Morty into a ruffled old crow," Liza said.

"It could happen," Howie told his friends. "Wizards have the power of transfiguration."

"What does a radio that runs off batteries have to do with a dirty crow?" Eddie asked.

Melody shook her head. "You're thinking of old-fashioned *transistor* radios. Howie is talking about something totally different."

"Transfiguration is the ability to change one thing into something else," Howie explained. "A wizard who wanted power could easily take over an entire city by changing all the people into animals. The animals would carry out her evil plans. I think that is exactly what Mrs. Jhick plans to do. Graduation would be the perfect time."

Eddie shook his head. "You really need a vacation. You've gone nuts."

"No, I know what I'm talking about," Howie said. "Mrs. Jhick turned poor Morty into a spying crow. She suspects that we know — that's why she's been watching us."

"Her glasses do make her eyes look big," Melody said slowly. "Do you think they could be magic glasses that help her spy on kids?"

Howie nodded. "But that's not the only way she keeps her evil eye on us. She also uses that necklace."

Liza hugged herself and shivered. "That amber stone looks like a giant eyeball. No matter where I stand, it stares right at me."

"And what about her name?" Howie said. "Don't you think it's odd?"

"Madge isn't so unusual," Melody argued. "I have an aunt whose name is Madge."

"You're right," Howie told her. "Madge isn't unusual by itself, but when you say it with her last name it changes. Try it."

"Madge Jhick," Liza said slowly.

"Faster," Howie urged.

"Madge Jhick, Madge Jhick," Melody said faster and faster until the two words blended together. "MadgeJhick."

"MAGIC!" Liza squealed. "Her name is *magic!*"

"Exactly," Howie said. "It all adds up."

"Yep, it adds up, all right," Eddie said. "It adds up to one, two, three friends who have lost their minds."

"But what if Howie is right?" Liza asked. "What if Madge Jhick is really planning to take over Bailey School at graduation?"

"Howie is not right," Eddie said. "A person cannot be turned into a bird, and an assistant principal cannot be a wizard, especially when she's a girl. Mrs. Jhick is not a wizard, and she can't make anybody do anything."

"Oh, yeah?" Howie asked. "Then tell Melody she's a nincompoop!"

"Gladly," Eddie said with a smirk. He turned to Melody. He opened his mouth. Nothing came out.

"See?" Howie said. "Mrs. Jhick cast a spell on you, and now you can't insult your friends."

Eddie put his hands on his cheeks. "This is horrible," Eddie gasped. "It's terrible. It's the end of the world. That wizette must be stopped!"

"I think it's great," Liza said with a giggle. "Just think, no more insults from Eddie — what's not to like?"

"Liza has a point," Melody said slowly. "It would be much nicer around Bailey School if Eddie never insulted anyone."

Howie grabbed Liza's and Melody's arms. "Remember, this is just a small bit of her magic. What if she changes all of us into crows?"

Liza looked at her fingers, imagining feathers in their place. "I don't think I'd like to be a bird," she said. "I'm afraid of heights."

"Then we'd better stop her," Howie said, slapping the trunk of the giant oak tree, "before we find ourselves living in this tree."

"Wait a minute," Eddie said. "You're jumping to conclusions. You don't know for sure Mrs. Jhick is a wizard."

"There's only one way to find out,"

Howie told him. "We'll follow her home after school. Then I'll be able to prove Mrs. Jhick is an evil wizard who plans on taking over Bailey School — and all of Bailey City!"

10

Now or Never

The next day the four kids were very careful to be well behaved. They didn't want Mrs. Jhick to notice them. Even Eddie didn't cause any trouble, except for when he blew bubbles in his milk at lunch.

After school they waited for Mrs. Jhick to leave. She stayed late, and the sun was already starting to set by the time she left the building. She carried a huge stack of books, and her long silver dress flowed around her ankles as she strode across the parking lot and down the street toward Bailey City Park.

"It's now or never," Howie said.

"Let's make it never," Eddie suggested, but Howie didn't hear him. Howie followed Mrs. Jhick, careful to stay within the shadows. Liza, Melody, and Eddie followed Howie.

Mrs. Jhick seemed to float through the park, along the trail that edged Swamp Dread. All the kids knew about the swamp. Some even believed a monster lived in its murky waters.

"I hope she stays out of the swamp," Melody murmured. "I don't think four kids can battle a swamp monster and a wicked wizard at once."

Eddie put up his fists. "Bring 'em on," he kidded. "I'll give them matching black eyes."

"Shh," Howie warned. "Or you'll be wearing black feathers like Morty."

As they skirted Swamp Dread, Liza glanced at the tangle of bushes and vines that lined the path. "It's the evil eye from Mrs. Jhick's necklace!" she yelped, pointing to a snarl of vines.

Four amber eyes glowed in the twilight. They stared straight at the four friends.

Melody inched closer to the vines before letting out a huge breath. "They're only cats," Melody assured her.

Sure enough, two cats, one black and one calico, scampered from the vines and disappeared into the shadows of the swamp.

The kids followed Mrs. Jhick all the way to a small cabin sitting alone on the edge of the swamp. A shed in the backyard leaned against a tall tree.

"Quick," Howie said, "hide!"

All four kids dashed behind trees, bushes, and rocks as Mrs. Jhick headed into the shed. It wasn't long before she strode out of the wooden door, crossed the backyard, and disappeared into the small cabin.

"What do you think she's doing?" Melody finally asked.

"She's probably baking brownies and knitting baby booties," Eddie said, rolling his eyes.

Howie waited another full minute before speaking. "I wonder what she keeps in that shed."

"There's only one way to find out," Eddie said. Before his friends could stop him, Eddie dashed across the yard and straight to the shed. Howie was close on his heels. Melody looked at Liza. Liza looked at Melody.

"We shouldn't go in there," Liza said.

"You're right," Melody said. "But I'm going anyway."

Liza sighed and followed Melody to the shed. Eddie slowly opened the door and the four friends peered inside. The small room was cool and smelled of dust. Liza batted away a cobweb in the doorway. A sliver of fading sunlight cast the inside of the shed in dim light.

"Aren't you going inside?" Howie asked Eddie.

"You're the one who wanted to see what was in here," Eddie snapped. "Why don't you go in?"

"You first," Howie said, giving Eddie a little push.

Before Eddie could take another step, a piercing cry cut through the darkening night.

"Scrwark!" Mortimer swooped down from a nearby tree.

"AAAAAAHHHHH!" Liza screeched and gave Melody a big shove. Melody bumped Howie. Howie fell against Eddie. Eddie tumbled into the dark shadows of Mrs. Jhick's shed.

Liza, Melody, and Howie hurried after Eddie. "That bird nearly scared my toenails off," Liza complained.

"If you think that's scary, wait until you see this," Eddie said, peeking under a canvas cover.

"What is it?" Howie whispered as he quietly closed the shed's door. The only light in the tiny room came from a small window.

Eddie jerked off the cover. As it fell to

the floor, Liza started to scream. Melody slapped her hand over Liza's mouth, cutting her scream short.

The four friends stared at a long row of cages. From inside each cage an animal peered out at them. There were at least a dozen rats, several lizards, three snakes, and one fat toad.

Howie slowly walked up to the cages. "Look," he whispered. "Each cage has a name on it."

Melody read the sign attached to one lizard's cage. "'Randy: won't eat spinach.'"

"'Lee,'" Liza read from a sign on a snake's aquarium. "'Doesn't follow directions.'"

Eddie put his nose next to a cage that held a big rat. "'Barbara: won't sit still,'" he read.

Howie gasped. "These aren't just animals. They're students from other schools. Mrs. Jhick turned them into animals!"

"But only the kids who acted bad,"

Liza whispered. "The sign on each cage tells what they did wrong."

"I don't like the looks of this," Melody said.

"Let's get out of here," Eddie said. He turned to leave, but he was too late.

A gust of wind blew open the door. Two cats, one black and one calico, darted inside. They weren't alone. Mrs. Jhick followed them.

11

Edward: Goofed Off
Too Much

"I see you've found my pupils," Mrs. Jhick said.

Howie gulped. "Pupils?" he asked. "You mean like eyeballs?"

Mrs. Jhick laughed. "Pupils, as in students. I call my pets my pupils because I'm teaching them to do tricks." Mrs. Jhick snapped her fingers. Mortimer flew in through the shed door and landed on Eddie's head.

Melody laughed, but Mrs. Jhick shook her head. "I haven't had Mortimer very long," Mrs. Jhick explained. "And he's a bit of a slow learner." Mrs. Jhick snapped her fingers again, and Mortimer landed on her shoulder.

"I do enjoy my animals," Mrs. Jhick

said. "They mind so much better than humans. Of course, I'm sure *you* children always follow the rules, don't you?"

Liza gulped. "I'm sorry we looked in your shed. We'd better get going." The kids raced past Mrs. Jhick and all the way to Melody's house.

"Whew!" Melody said when the kids were safe on her porch. "That was close. I thought Mrs. Jhick was going to turn us into birds."

Eddie shook his head. "Naw, not a chance. I sure wish I had one of those rats that do tricks, though. I wonder if my grandmother will let me get one."

"If you don't watch out," Howie told Eddie, "you'll *be* one of those rats."

Liza nodded. "And the label on the cage will read 'Edward: goofed off too much.'"

"Speaking of goofing off," Eddie said, "that's exactly what I'm going to do tomorrow at school. It's the last week of the school year — the perfect time to goof off a little."

"No!" Melody shouted. "If Mrs. Jhick really is a wizard, it could be the end of you."

"We have to be good," Howie said. "I've figured it all out. Mrs. Jhick can only use kids who don't behave to carry out her evil plans. If we are all good, Mrs. Jhick will have to leave Bailey School because there won't be enough bad kids for her to turn into animals."

"If we're good," Eddie argued, "we won't be having any fun. And if there's one thing I plan to do, it's to have fun!"

The next day at school, Eddie went into goof-off mode. He didn't do his work. He sang songs during art class and drew pictures during music. Instead of playing basketball in PE, he played kick-ball. Finally, on Friday afternoon, Coach Ellison sent Eddie to the assistant princi-pal's office. Eddie never came back.

12

Eddie the Rat

Melody, Liza, and Howie waited under the oak tree for a long time after school. Eddie didn't show up.

"I hope Eddie is all right," Melody said.

"We'll see him tomorrow morning at graduation," Liza said. "We can find out what trouble he got into then."

But the next morning, Eddie wasn't at the graduation ceremony. Liza squeezed her hands together as Mrs. Jhick gave the graduation speech. "What if Mrs. Jhick turned Eddie into a rat?" Liza whispered to Melody. "Maybe Eddie has little whiskers now instead of freckles."

Melody giggled. "I think that would be an improvement." Liza didn't laugh. She looked ready to cry.

"Come on," Howie suggested when everyone was having cake and punch.

"Let's go to Mrs. Jhick's office. Maybe we'll find a clue about Eddie."

The kids tiptoed down the tile hallway. They eased open Mrs. Jhick's office door to find . . . nothing.

"It's totally empty!" Liza squealed. "What did she do with Eddie?"

"Maybe he's in her shed," Melody said.

"We have to find out," Howie said. The kids turned around to run, but they didn't get far.

"What are you kids doing?" Principal Davis asked, scratching his bald head.

"We . . . uh . . . we were looking for Mrs. Jhick," Liza said.

"Sorry," Mr. Davis told the kids. "She left right after her speech. She won't be back. She's gone to another school district."

"Gone?" Melody said with a gulp.

"Do you know where she went?" Liza asked anxiously.

Principal Davis shook his bald head. "No, she didn't leave a forwarding address. But it's very nice that you kids care about her. She said this school was filled with nothing but good kids."

"Thanks," Howie said with his head bowed. The kids didn't say anything until they stopped outside under the oak tree.

"Well," Melody said. "Our plan sort of worked. We did get rid of Mrs. Jhick by behaving."

"Except for Eddie," Liza said sadly. "We may never see him again."

Howie sat down on the ground. "I'll never let my dad set another rat trap as long as I live."

"Eddie may have been a tease, but he was still a good friend. I can't believe he's gone," Liza said. A tear trickled down her cheek.

Melody's eyes were teary, too. "If Eddie would just come back, I might even let him win a race."

"You wouldn't have to," Eddie said, coming up behind Melody. "I could beat you with my eyes closed."

"Eddie!" Liza squealed. "You're not a rat!"

"No," Eddie said with a laugh. "But I am a winner." Eddie held up a soccer trophy. "My grandmother let me play in the camp's tournament. She said it was my first commitment and the team needed me."

"We thought you had been turned into a rat by the wizard," Howie said.

"What wizard?" Eddie asked.

"Mrs. Jhick, of course," Melody said.

Eddie rolled his eyes. "I told you, women can*not* be wizards."

"Can too," Melody snapped and chased Eddie around the playground.

"Oh, no," Liza said. "Here we go again."

Howie shook his head. "I'm not sure what happened today. I don't know if wizards can be assistant principals. I don't even know if wizards wear graduation gowns, but I do know that it takes more than a wizard to make Eddie behave!"